The Wacky Field Day

Dr. Linda McCallister

Illustrated by Connie McCallister Jordan

The Wacky Field Day
Copyright © 2023 by Linda McCallister

First Edition

Hardcover ISBN: 979-8-8229-1513-8
Paperback ISBN: 979-8-8229-1514-5

Dedicated to:

My children and grandchildren, all of whom are gifted.

Notes: I have used the names of my children, grandchildren, family members, and friends throughout this and other works. The descriptions, personalities, and actions of my characters are fiction and do not represent those members of my family or friends, especially since these characters are 3rd through 5th graders and the real people for whom they are named are much older. At times a character may have something in common with the family member or friend, such as Konnor being a gymnast or Zane being in plays, but this is not always the case, and more often, there is only one thing my characters might have in common with those having the same name. The names are purely to honor them.

With permission, I have included the characters in the late A. Jean Triplett's book, <u>Not My Max</u>, and in all my books in this series, <u>The Magical Gingerbread House</u>, <u>The Astonishing Time Machine</u>, and <u>The Wacky Field Day</u>. I will continue to keep her characters in future books as well.

Special thanks to my sister and illustrator, Connie McCallister Jordan. Special thanks also to Zane Absten for helpful thoughts on this plot, and my editors: Cheryl Rogers, Cole McClain, Connie McCallister Jordan, Lorinda McClain, and Tiffany Murphy.

The Students in Mrs. Williams' Class

Tiffany, Paul, Lorinda

Zane, Grace, Hannah, Hayden,
Alexandra

Emma, Corwin, Joelyn

Konnor, Liv, Deuce, Cole

Chapter 1

Konnor always dreamed of going to the Olympics and winning the gold medal in gymnastics. It wasn't the dream of most other girls her age, but then she was a very determined young lady and willing to work hard to make her dream come true. Her parents did all they could to help her keep her dream alive. She spent hours in the gym practicing, making her skills perfect. Konnor had been athletic since birth. She could walk at 6 ½ months. She would watch her older sister and try to do the things her sister was doing in gymnastics. After she begged her mom for lessons, her mom let her enroll in gymnastics at 16 months. By 18 months she could already walk across a balance beam. At 20 months she could do backbend kickovers. A couple of coaches had tried to get her to move to their gyms when she was only four years old. When her parents took her to meets out of state, more coaches would try to get her to move to their gyms so they could coach her. Then, when she started attending camps, she began meeting even more coaches, ones who had coached some American Olympians. As she grew older, Konnor began to make friends with some of the girls who were famous in gymnastics.

Third grade was the last year Konnor would be a full-time student in her school. She had already reached level 8 while most gymnasts her age were on a level 4 or lower. She did that over the summer, before school started. Konnor had several goals. She wanted to reach the Elite level. She wanted to be on the Junior National Team and eventually on the Senior National Team. The National Team goes all over the World to compete. Konnor wanted to compete in other countries. Konnor also hoped to one day be America's National Champion. Konnor was working hard to reach her goals. This was the way to reach her ultimate goal, the Olympics.

While only 2% of all gymnasts will compete at the Elite level, even fewer make the national teams. Getting to go to the Olympic trial would be a dream come true, but being on the actual Olympic team was her actual goal, and she was working hard to do just that!

Konnor had lived, eaten, and breathed gymnastics for as long as she could remember. She just knew that her journey to the Olympics meant she had to reach the Elite level as soon as she could. She and her parents knew that if her dreams were to come true, she would soon have to begin training more hours each day. Her coach and parents began to talk about Konnor attending half day at school, training, and then doing home schooling after training.

She was a mature young lady in most areas of her life. Konnor still liked to ride her bicycle, play with her favorite doll, bake brownies, and play the games other 3rd graders play. Unlike most children her age, Konnor was beginning to also think about what she would do after gymnastics when she was a lot older. Last year Konnor had heard the girls at camp who were in high school talk about what they would do after gymnastics, so she began to think about becoming a doctor. She thought it might be good to treat gymnasts who got injured since there are lots of injuries in gymnastics. While Konnor was a talented gymnast, she was also a smart young lady who could become a doctor. In fact, she was a student in Mrs. Williams' gifted class. She really enjoyed the research and projects she got to do in Mrs. Williams' class for gifted students. However, she couldn't wait to begin training six hours a day, six days a week!

Chapter 2

Zane was another student in Mrs. Williams' class for gifted students. He was a big collector of baseball cards. Zane also loved being in plays and movies and was both good enough and cute enough to be the star in any performance. All the students in her class loved being around Zane because he knew how to make people feel great. He could talk with anybody, children or adults. When Zane was with someone, he always wanted to leave them happy. That was one of his many talents. He loved making others feel special, like they could do anything they wanted to do.

Just before Spring Break, Zane found out that his mother was very sick and needed some expensive medicine to keep her from getting even sicker. He was worried about his mother and wanted to help, but he didn't know how. He knew she was worried about the cost of her medicine. He needed to take away some of her worry and make her happy. Zane just knew he had to find a way.

Zane lived just a few houses away from Mrs. Williams. He sometimes played with her children, Sarah and Sam, and their dog, Max. Mrs. Williams found out that Zane's mother was sick. She went to visit Zane's mom and took her a wonderful meal for the family. While there, she could see that Zane was worried. She tried to comfort Zane. Then, she realized Zane was worried about more than just his mom's health. He was also worried about the cost of her medicine and medical bills. She asked Zane's mother if she would mind if Zane helped her by walking and feeding her dog over the weekend, unless of course, she needed him to take care of her. Mrs. Williams explained that she and her family were going to visit her parents. Zane loved the idea and was very happy when Mrs. Williams told him she would pay him. Because it was Mrs. Williams, he told her he would do it for free, but Mrs. Williams insisted.

The first time Zane went to Mrs. Williams' house to walk and feed her dog Max, when he used the key she left him to unlocked the door and open it. . . Surprise! The dog ran out the door and just kept running. Zane didn't want to tell anyone that Max ran away, so he started searching for him. He looked all over the neighborhood. Zane walked to the school, the pool area, and a nearby church to search for the dog. No Max. He was so worried. He didn't know what Mrs. Williams would say. Zane also thought about how sad Sarah and Sam would be. He had to find Max so they could all be happy.

Zane finally decided to put his search for the runaway dog online. It was only a few minutes later that a neighbor answered, showed a picture of Max, and said the dog was safe at her house. The lady who found Max knew it was Mrs. Williams' dog and offered to meet Zane to return the dog. Zane was so relieved. He fed Max but didn't need to walk him since the dog had been running throughout the neighborhood for close to an hour. Zane was surprised because he knew that Max had caused a lot of trouble in the past, but lately had been a very good and helpful dog. After that, when Zane went to feed or walk the dog, Max was very good. Max never ran away from Zane again.

Chapter 3

Mrs. Williams' class had been studying India. Students had researched and presented their information along with a project on several areas of Indian life and culture. There was only one presentation left on Tuesday before they would go on to learn about another country.

The presentation Emma was giving was on the four major religions of India. She had a power point that talked about the four religions, and she passed out brochures she had made for each student. Before Emma told them there were about 4200 religions in the world, she told them her mother was from Taiwan and was Buddhist. That is why she signed up to talk about the religions of India. Most of the students in Mrs. Williams' class were of the Christian religion and knew very little about other religions. She told the class that of the seven most popular religions in the world, three of India's four major religions were included in the seven. She started out explaining a little about Hinduism and Buddhism, then she finished up by telling them about Sikhism and Jainism.

Emma told the class, "Hinduism is the third largest religion in the world with over a billion followers. Does anyone know which religion has the most followers?" Paul said, "The Christian religion is number one. They have over 2 billion followers." Zane said, "I was Joseph in a play called 'Joseph and His Coat of Many Colors'. Most Christians have heard that story. And I think it's also in the Hebrew Bible."

After Emma explained more about Hinduism, she went on to talk about Buddhism which was founded by Buddha and originated about 2500 years ago. People who study religions tell us that Buddhism originated partly from Hindu religious traditions. Grace said, "Wow! That is such a long time ago."

When she finished talking about Buddhism, Emma asked if anyone had questions or comments about either of those two religions. Lorinda asked, "Do I really get good luck or become rich if I rub Buddha's stomach?" Emma explained, "When the Buddha who founded the religion died, Buddhism split into two different parts. The Laughing Buddha is a Chinese Buddhist monk who is not the Buddha of the Indian religion. It is said that rubbing the stomach of that Buddha statue can bring you luck, happiness, and riches." Zane asked, "Where can I get one of those statues because I could use some luck, happiness, and riches right now?" The class broke out in laughter.

Konnor spoke up and told the class, "My grandfather is Muslim, and like the preacher or priest of his church, only they call him an Imam." Emma told the class that different religions not only have different names for their preachers, but some religions also have different names for their God.

Emma continued her presentation by telling the class about Sikhism, a religion that became a faith in 1699. It is one of the youngest major religions. She told the class more about the Sikhs, their beliefs, and their traditions before she moved on to tell them about Jainism.

"Jainism is also one of the world's oldest religions, and like Buddhism, is about 2500 years old and originated in India. Most people who study religions think that although Hinduism, Buddhism, and Jainism are about 2500 years old, the Jain religion might be a little older than the Hindu religion. However, some people think Hinduism is the oldest." Then Grace said, "Wow! I thought 2500 years for Hinduism was old, and now I find out that Jainism might be a tad bit older than Hinduism! Wonder if there is a religion that is older?"

Emma told them they should do some research because she didn't know. Paul found out that there was a religion called Ajivika that is mentioned in the writings of Buddhism and Jainism, but it no longer exists. After their research Emma went on with her presentation.

She continued telling the class about Jainism. The thing the class found most interesting from her whole presentation was in her next statements. "They do not believe in violence, which means not harming any living thing, including plants and animals. This means not even stepping on an ant. They are vegetarians, but they don't eat root vegetables like carrots and potatoes because a person could harm small insects in the ground when getting the vegetables out of the ground. Jains even cover their mouths to prevent killing any living thing that might accidently fly into their mouths." Then she added, "It does happen. Some of you may have seen that a popular singer once swallowed an insect during a performance."

Several students covered their mouths when they heard this. Lorinda said, "I'll never see bugs the same way again. I learned so much that I never knew. I think this is one of the best presentations, although it would be hard to beat the time machine presentation." The class agreed.

Chapter 4

After the last presentation on India, Mrs. Williams was ready to begin with their studies of Canada. But first, she asked students if any of them would like Nathaniel's new address. Nathaniel had moved to Washington, D.C. with his mom and dad and had promised to send his former classmates his new address. Grace said, "I wish we could write to him this very minute." Alexandra added, "We sure do miss him. I want to write to him too." Even Corwin, who started attending Mrs. Williams' class after Nathaniel moved, said, "Nathaniel went to my church. I miss him too."

"Okay," Mrs. Williams relented. "I was just going to pass out his address, but I will give you a few minutes to write a quick note to Nathaniel. I will even mail all your letters in one envelope to him. Oh, and speaking of writing, I have a surprise for one of you. Joelyn, not only did you win the school writing competition, but your story will also be in tomorrow's edition of the newspaper."

After the letters to Nathaniel were turned in, Mrs. Williams finally began to talk about Canada. Students were studying countries of the world and had already studied England, France, Germany, Mexico, Russia, and India. They were excited to study Canada because it was close to the United States. Some of them had been to Canada with their families. Konnor was excited to learn more about Canada because she knew the Junior National Team would be going to Canada.

Mrs. Williams began with the geography of Canada. Students each selected a topic and began by researching a province, territory, or capital city. Students were to write a report about their area before giving an oral report. This presentation was to be different from the reports they did. Mrs. Williams set up a portable green screen, pulled up a map of Canada on her computer to show on the green screen, and told her students they were going to be weatherpersons. They were to do further research on the weather in the province or territory or city they had researched for their report. Then, they would write a script for their weather report, being sure to give a little information about their location. Mrs. Williams gave them an example, "If it was during a time when there was a gymnastics meet and Konnor was giving a report on her research about the weather in British Columbia, she might start by saying, 'Here in Richmond, at British Columbia's Olympic Oval Arena, the weather will be cold, but bright and sunny as gymnasts from all over the country travel to The Canadian National Championships for the meet held this weekend.' She would then give the exact temperatures and weather patterns." Mrs. Williams informed them that she would tape them and show them the tapes of their reports after everyone had presented. After lunch, students began their research and then spent the rest of the day researching, writing reports, and writing their scripts for the weather reports.

WE SHOULD RESPECT
ALL PEOPLE OF ALL
RACES AND RELIGIONS!

Chapter 5

A few days after the presentation on religions, Mrs. Williams saw some students in the hallway and lunchroom approach Emma in a way she didn't like. No one had ever seen Mrs. Williams angry before, but boy, was she angry now! She spoke to those students about their behavior, but she decided she also needed to say something to her class. What she had seen was very disturbing. After Emma told the class about her mom being a Buddhist and then talked about the Laughing Buddha, her classmates discussed it with other friends. These students would walk past Emma or go up to her and rub their stomachs, making fun of her.

Mrs. Williams also heard about some of the gymnasts who were making comments to Konnor when she went to practice. This was very upsetting to Mrs. Williams. While she was upset, she was more afraid it would soon be students at school making these comments. She could not allow that to happen.

So, the Tuesday after Emma's presentation, Mrs. Williams began class by asking her students how they would feel if someone said bad things about their skin color or religion. She said she had seen and heard that some students in this class were experiencing others saying bad things to them. A person's religion is very important to them. A person's skin color is an important part of who they are. Plus, you never know what a person is going through. Being different should be a good thing. We can learn from those who are not like us. They may not look like you, but that should be okay. They may believe differently yet be very religious. I know that makes them very sad to hear some students say mean things to them.

Several students made comments about how wrong that was. They all agreed that they wouldn't want someone to treat them that way, and if they saw that happening, either at school or at another place, they would speak up and defend their friend. Mrs. Williams knew her students were saying what they should say, but she wasn't sure some of them meant they would really speak up if a friend was getting bullied. However, after the class discussed this, Mrs. Williams wrote on the white board: WE SHOULD RESPECT ALL PEOPLE OF ALL RACES AND RELIGIONS!

These smart students all knew why Mrs. Williams was talking to them. During the remainder of the class, students seemed to be especially nice to Emma and Konnor. Some even told the girls how sorry they were that other kids were being mean to them.

Chapter 6

When the town leaders heard about a bicycle event to raise money for a children's hospital that gave them an idea. Over spring break, they wanted to have a bicycle event in their town. The organizers wanted this to be a bicycle ride for children though. Children would get sponsors and then ride around a huge church parking lot. Each ride around the lot would be worth $1. When several members of the area churches and businesses heard about the event, they wanted to be the sponsors for the children.

Konnor and her friends, including Zane, signed up for this fund raiser. It would be a fun way to help the community. Zane secretly wished that they had a fund raiser for people like his mom, but he was happy that so many children would be helped. He would just have to help his mom by himself.

On the day of event, they all brought their bikes to the church parking lot and began to ride when the announcer said "GO!" The least number of circles around the lot was made by a 4-year-old who made it around the parking lot 20 times. Konnor and most of her friends biked a hundred times around the parking lot, the maximum allowed. Since there were so many riders, the hospital was going to get a lot of money from this charity event!

There were cameras everywhere to take pictures of the event. The children didn't realize people other than their parents would be taking pictures since they were just riding their bikes.

When the bike riders were all finished, the church that hosted the event had a big cook out for the children and their families. Churches are known for their pot-luck dinners and many members brought side dishes. Grills were set up for meat and homemade ice cream was planned for dessert. The children got to help turn the cranks of the ice cream machines that weren't electric. Konnor and her grandma made their famous chocolate chip brownies. What a great day!

That evening, Konnor and her friends were on the 6:00 news. The next morning there was an article with pictures in the newspaper. The children all felt that they had gotten their "15 minutes of fame." Nobody but Konnor and Zane had ever had their pictures in the newspaper or on TV before.

As it happened, Konnor had won the all-around gold medal in a recent gymnastics meet. A reporter interviewed her after the meet and the interview was shown on television just two days earlier. The TV reporter mentioned that one of the bike riders was the gymnast that they had just reported on a couple of days ago. Then, they showed her doing part of her beam routine and winning the gold again.

Her mom had also filmed her when she was three years old doing a beam routine before judges. It was her very first judged routine which was put on the internet. Someone reposted that video.

Chapter 7

As the children began to enter the classroom after spring break, Mrs. Williams couldn't believe her eyes! Not only was Hannah's long hair now cut short, Grace had dyed her hair brown, and Liv now had streaks of blonde in her hair. But the biggest surprise was Hayden. He had dyed his hair white! Even Mrs. Williams did a double take. Then, she jokingly said, "I think I have some new students in my class that I have never met. Do we need to introduce them?" Students roared with laughter.

Before class started, the children asked Konnor what it was like to be famous. Konnor said, "I'm not famous. We were all in the newspaper and on TV." But the children had seen the interviews. Most of them had also seen the internet beam routine of 3-year-old Konnor that had been reposted over spring break.

Joelyn was the first to notice that the newspaper article of the story she had written was posted on one of the bulletin boards in the class. She was surprised and thrilled to see it there. Mrs. Williams told her, "You can take the article home if you want."

Students took a few minutes to review the research and scripts they had completed before the break. After the weather reports and the showing of the tapes, the students made lots of comments. Some thought they did a nice job, but a few didn't like what they saw. "I should have spoken a little clearer." "Someone should have told me my hair was messed up." "I wish I had worn something else." Mrs. Williams just laughed. "Do you think the weatherpersons on TV think about these kinds of things? If you decide to become a weatherperson, please come back and tell me the answer."

Then, the class began learning more about Canada. They learned about the controversy over the Father of Hockey and Wayne Gretzky who was the greatest hockey player ever. Some students had heard that he quit hockey to move back to California and spend time with his family. However, no one in class knew that he had some medical problems. "It's sad that so many athletes have injuries or health issues," said Konnor. Then she added, "I hope I never have these problems."

They discussed Newton's Laws of Motion and how those laws applied to hockey. After that, students discussed terms that Deuce heard when he had gone to his friend Graig's game. Deuce was new to this sport since there weren't many teams in West Virginia. Mrs. Williams gave her students a few minutes to research hockey terms and discuss them. Her students found several terms used in hockey such as hat trick and deke. When someone said "hoser" was a term used, Mrs. Williams said she'd better not hear anyone use that term, as she knew there were no losers in the whole school. "Everyone is a winner of something, even if it's just spreading love. Everyone can make our World a better place." Then she wrote on the board: EVERYONE IS THE WINNER OF SOMETHING!

Then, students researched the rules, the physical requirements of hockey, how hockey sticks were made, and the math and physics of hockey. For the last activity of the day, Mrs. Williams had set up one of the tables to test the physics of the game. With a small goal on each end of the table, they used a small, round, black rubber piece as a puck and the wooden sticks from inside of new shoes that were shaped like hockey sticks. Students took turns playing before they discussed the physics of hockey. They could see how their games might differ if they had played on actual ice. It was a busy day, and even Mrs. Williams was surprised they did so much in one day.

Chapter 8

Santa brought Konnor a special doll for Christmas. Her mom had just ordered her an outfit for the doll. It was Konnor's favorite outfit of all the clothes she now had for her doll. The doll's outfit was an Olympic outfit. It was a red, white, and blue leotard that even included three medals. She fixed the doll's hair to look like her hair. It was her favorite doll and she loved it. One day she took the doll with her to the gym to show the other girls. Then, she put it in her locker. The lockers didn't have locks. When she got ready to go home, she opened her locker to get her doll and other things.

Her doll was missing!

Earlier, a couple of the girls had said mean things to her about her being black and her dad being a Muslim, but this seemed even meaner. These girls had said things before, but they were worse today. Konnor wondered if they were the ones who took her doll. Konnor was so sad. They searched all the lockers and the rest of the gym, but no doll. Most of the girls had already left the gym before Konnor even opened her locker because she had been talking with her coach for a few minutes after class. Konnor had to leave without her doll.

The next day when she went to the gym, the coach asked the group if anyone knew what happened to Konnor's doll. Everyone was silent. Then the coach told them, "If you were the one who took her doll and we find it, you will be in big trouble. That doll is a collector's item and worth a lot of money. We can call the police, but we would rather not." Still there was only silence.

The very next day, Konnor hoped that whoever took her doll would return it. They did not.

Tuesday in class, when Konnor was talking with Zane, she told him about her missing doll. Then she saw Mrs. Williams close by, so she said to Zane, "Shh. The teacher will hear. This happened at the gym not here at school. I don't know if one of the girls who was saying mean things was the same person who took my doll."

Mrs. Williams had heard them talking about the missing doll. She pretended not to hear, but she saw how sad Konnor was. Her husband just happened to be a police officer. He turned up at the gym in uniform and spoke to Konnor's coach that very afternoon. The girls were wide-eyed at seeing a policeman. After he left, the gymnasts were concerned. They wanted to know if he was there about the doll. Their coach replied, "What do you think? I warned you if the doll was not returned someone would be in big trouble, did I not?"

The very next day, Konnor's doll showed up in the gym bathroom. One of the other coaches found it in the cabinet under the sink when she went to get a new roll of toilet paper. Konnor was not the only happy child. Everyone clapped with delight.

Konnor laughed. She knew she might never have gotten her doll back if the policeman had not come to the gym. Konnor wondered if the girl who took her doll knew that the policeman was Mrs. Williams' husband. She also wondered if Mrs. Williams had asked him to go to the gym in uniform. At that moment, Konnor didn't care who took her doll. She was just happy to have her favorite doll back. Her coach told Konnor that she thought that whoever took her doll was just jealous, not only of her having such a great doll, but also of Konnor's talent. The coach then told Konnor that she had a secret. She would only tell Konnor if Konnor promised to never ever tell. Konnor promised. The policeman was only there to ask about signing up his daughter, Sarah, for lessons.

That was the last time Konnor was bullied at the gym. Slowly the word got out that she was indeed famous. More children watched the internet of little Konnor and her beam routine. The mean kids at the gym knew about her winning gold medals. The ones who had missed the TV and news reports began hearing about them. Instead of not liking that she was different or being jealous of her, they started to respect her and wanted to be her friend. Konnor didn't yet know that the bullying had stopped and still dreaded going to the gym some days. Sometimes she would think about the mean things they had said earlier and her doll that was taken. It would cause her to lose her focus and mess up. Once while thinking of the mean things some of them had said and of her missing doll, she fell off the beam. She rarely fell off, and it was a miracle she didn't get hurt because the way she landed was not good. She had always felt gymnastics was so much fun. It just wasn't as much fun anymore.

Chapter 9

A few days later, after a pouring rainfall from the previous night, the gym was closed because of a leaky roof. The leaky roof had caused parts of the gym to be flooded. A repair crew was coming in. There was no school for students on that very day because of teacher meetings and training. Students were happy that their day off had turned out to be a warm, sunny day. Konnor, as always, stayed busy. She had a lot of interests and things she was good at doing. She knew she would have to quit doing some of her favorite things once she started her gymnastics training for so many hours. However, for now, she was doing as many of her favorite things as possible. Today was one of those days she wanted to spend some time drawing and painting.

Sometimes she would paint something outside that she could see or imagine. Other times, she would paint something that would show her mood for the day. Then, there were times that she would do drawings. Today she started with a painting of her doll on a canvas. Next, she painted a more modern painting with lines going every way and a star in one corner. Then she decided to get her sketch book out and once more pretend that she was a designer. She was slowly filling her sketchbook with leotard designs. Konnor knew that some of the famous gymnasts designed their own leotards, and she wanted to design her leotard one day. She was a talented artist for her age.

Just as she was finishing her second leotard design, her grandma called to see if she was doing anything special on her day off from school and the gym. Konnor was always busy if she wasn't at school or the gym, but she was never too busy to help around the house. She liked helping on her day off, and she helped around her house and at her grandma's house. She was good at organizing things like her grandma's sock drawer or her pantry. Today she asked her grandma if she could scrub her shower. She hadn't done that before, but she knew she could do it. Also, grandma always gave her some money for the jobs she did, and Konnor wanted to save for a pet bunny.

Then, Konnor asked if she and her brother could plant the flowers that her grandma had bought. Her grandma agreed. After the flowers were planted, they spread some mulch. With the money, Konnor had enough to buy the bunny she wanted. She also needed a cage and some food for the bunny. Her brother wanted to buy a new video game.

Chapter 10

On Tuesday, Mrs. Williams informed the class that there was to be a field day at the end of the year and her classes were to help plan for it. With her help, her students were to sign up teachers to sponsor each event and plan where each event would take place. Students would need to sign up for a sport. If buses were needed, they were to fill out the forms to order them and get parent permissions.

First, the class began to brainstorm about all the things they needed to do to make the field day successful. Mrs. Williams had mentioned a few, but they knew there was much more to do than what she told them. The students made a list of all the jobs that needed to be done. Then, they divided the class into small groups that would do each of the jobs. They needed to send a letter to each teacher in the building to see what group each teacher wanted to sponsor. It should include a form for them to return. The form should also ask each teacher to list how many students could sign up for the sport they were going to sponsor. Students looked at their list of sports and made sure to add sports that students with disabilities could do. Then, when they looked at the list of the sponsoring teachers, they realized that they needed more volunteers. The PTA was glad to help. When they got the forms back from the teachers, they would make a list with the locations for each event.

Mrs. Williams' students thought it might be good to post each teacher's name and sport. Then, it would be easier for students to see what they wanted to do on field day. It would also help them keep track of who signed up to play each sport and who needed permission slips.

Mrs. Williams told them that the PTA had money to help with expenses. They wanted to hire an ice cream truck to give a free cone to each student, teacher, and parent volunteer. That meant that each person would need a coupon to get their free cone. If students were going somewhere other than the school, they would be able to get their treat after they returned to the school. Another job was added to their list. They would need to count and sort coupons and put them in each teacher's mailbox.

That made the students think about lunches for the students who would be some place other than the school. They added the job of working with the cafeteria cooks to get them to make bag lunches for those students. They also needed to schedule lunch time for each sport since students that stayed at school would not be with their regular teachers.

The students wondered if they should give awards or mention students or groups of students who deserved special recognition. Corwin's dad was mayor. Maybe he could come at the end of the day for an assembly. He could give a short speech and recognize students that did well and groups that played each other and won, like football or basketball teams. Corwin said he would ask his dad if he would be able to come to speak at the assembly.

Hannah thought about safety. She thought they should have a first aid station that included the nurse, but also a couple of parent volunteers who would be available to help students get to the nurse's station, go after ice, or do whatever was needed.

The class continued to think of all the jobs that needed to be done. Mrs. Williams told them that between now and next week they should continue to think of the jobs they would need to do before the field day. Today, in the remaining class time, they should break into their groups to begin specific planning for the jobs that needed to be done immediately.

Once the class broke into groups to work on the various parts of the planning process, classmates in her group told Konnor she was sure to be recognized for her gymnastics. Konnor said, "I don't know if I'm going to sign up for gymnastics." Zane asked, "Why?" Konnor shrugged her shoulders but didn't answer. Zane continued, "You've just lost your confidence because you messed up a time or two. You are the greatest gymnast I know!" Konnor just said, "I don't know." Then she whispered to Zane, "That's not it." Konnor sadly shared her feelings, "Some of the kids from the gym will be there. They made comments to me about my race and my dad's and grandpa's religion. I keep remembering that someone even stole my favorite doll from my locker. I used to be so happy at the gym, but now, although I'm happy to have my doll back, I'm just sad when I go to the gym. I mess up more than ever when I practice my skills. It's hard to focus which is why I'm messing up. I'm just feeling like maybe I shouldn't even continue with my gymnastics anymore."

After school, Zane was talking with Deuce while walking to the buses. That's when Deuce mentioned that although he used to be good at baseball, he had struck out during his last game. Zane knew Deuce was sad because he felt like he had let his teammates down. Zane had an idea, a way to help his mom and help his friends too. What if he could make kids feel more confident and realize that mistakes in one game don't mean that they are not good? It just means they had a bad day. After all, everyone has a bad day every now and then. No one is perfect. Zane told Deuce, "I have something that guarantees you will do well in your games. But, it costs a little money." If Deuce could bring him some money, Zane would give him some of his 'magic pops.' Deuce asked, "Do they really work?" Zane replied, "Of course. Why do you think I always do so well that I get parts in plays?"

Deuce said, "Maybe you better bring enough for Liv. She's a great player, but she messed up in her last softball game. She threw the bat twice and got ejected from the game." "Sure," agreed Zane. "Bring her money too."

Zane knew that the 'magic pops' were not magic. They were just regular candy, but he knew that selling them would mean more money for his mom's medicine. It would also make Deuce and Liv have more confidence and play better ball. Everyone would be happy.

The next day, before school started, Zane saw Deuce. He was with Liv. They each gave him money and he gave them his 'magic pops.' Zane explained about the 'magic pops.' "Each bag has 4 pieces that you should eat about an hour before your games. They have kind of a snap to them and taste so good. The red one is for long-lasting energy, and the yellow one is for quick energy. The blue one helps you focus on the game, while the green one I call the 'I can do it pop.'"

About an hour before their games, they ate the 'magic pops.' They both did well in the games they played that day. They told Zane the next day how well they played, and how they wanted to buy more 'magic pops' for their next games. Soon, other students found out about the 'magic pops' and wanted them too. Zane was only too happy to sell them some 'magic pops.' He sold his candy to so many students that he was sure he could help his mom now. Then he remembered Emma and Konnor. Emma was standing nearby, so Zane was able to ask her right then and there. She agreed to buy some the next day. Now Zane wanted to find Konnor. He thought she could use some confidence. Zane wanted to help her with his 'magic pops.' He knew she had been bullied with racial comments and had even fallen during her last beam routine. He wondered if she might need some of his 'magic pops.'

Chapter 11

Zane sold his 'magic pops' to other students during the next few days. Cole decided to pull a prank on Zane. Cole didn't pull as many pranks on his friends anymore. He didn't want anyone to feel as bad as he felt when he thought about Hayden and the time machine. Cole asked if he could buy some of the 'magic pops.' "Of course," Zane agreed. Cole said he would go ahead and give Zane the money today, and just get the candy next week. Zane hadn't gotten the money ahead of giving his friends the 'magic pops' before, but he agreed and took Cole's money. Zane knew this would allow him to buy more of the candy to sell to all his friends.

That evening, Zane went to the store to buy more pops. When he handed the store clerk his money, the clerk called the manager over. The money was fake. The manager called the police. Just then, Zane put his hand in his pocket. He found an envelope in his pocket with something inside. There was money, real money, in the envelope. A note was also in the envelope. It said, "Sorry, you've been pranked. Here is the real money to pay for my 'magic pops'. Have a great day!"

Zane was sure Cole was laughing now, but he wondered how Cole had been able to put the envelope in his pocket without him knowing. He showed the store manager the note. The store manager was surprised, but since he knew Cole, he laughed. He called the police to tell them that it was just a mix up, and then he let Zane pay for the pops and go home. Zane was relieved that he didn't get in trouble with the police, and even more relieved that no one found out he was buying regular candy and selling them as 'magic pops.'

Chapter 12

The next week, students in Mrs. Williams's class couldn't wait to get the forms back. Mr. Rogers, the math teacher, was the first to respond. He wanted to sponsor the golf group. Then Ms. Browning, who was the P.E. teacher, handed in two papers. One was for her, and the second one was for the other P.E. teacher, Mrs. Kiser. Each would sponsor a soccer team to play against each other. During class that morning, other forms were given to the class. Now they could begin to plan for the specifics of the events.

Students thought about the day and knew there would have to be travel time to and from some events and eating time. They decided that all competitions would begin in the afternoon while the morning hours would be spent practicing and learning the rules of the games if students didn't already know them. For instance, those going to the gymnastics competition could have an 'open gym' before the judges came in for the meet. For ball teams, they could scrimmage. For archery, they could practice on balloon boards.

The principal, Mrs. Lohan, came into the class. She said the parent newsletter would include an article about the field day before asking the students for any information they wanted included in the article. The students asked Mrs. Williams and Mrs. Lohan what they thought about all groups practicing in the morning with competitions in the afternoon after lunch. They both thought that this was a great plan. Mrs. Lohan said she would put the info in the staff memo this week. Then Mrs. Lohan added that she would also include a form in the parent newsletter asking for volunteers. Tiffany said, "Thank you. Two less things that need to be done by our class." Before she left the classroom, the principal told them what a great job they were doing, and if they needed anything else from her, to let her know.

Corwin said he had asked his dad, and his dad said he would be happy to speak at the assembly. Mrs. Lohan was thrilled and told him she would contact the mayor to give him more information.

As the class was discussing the parent newsletter article, their plans, and the location of each event, Alexandra suddenly had an idea. She suggested that maybe she should contact the local newspaper to see if she could write an article about the field day. She knew the people there because she had written articles for them before. She could even write before-the-event and after-the-event articles.

Students reviewed the list of sports, sponsoring teachers, and locations they made:

1) Table Tennis – Mr. Hanks – lobby
2) Fishing – Mr. Bass – need bus – at the lake
3) Swimming – Mrs. Scott – at the pool next to the school football field
4) Football – Mr. McClain and Mr. Cole – the Middle School football field
5) Basketball – Mr. Brannon and Mrs. Jordan – boys' gym
6) Track and Field – Mr. Chandler – track field
7) Tennis – Miss Absten – school tennis courts
8) Rowing – Need bus – Mrs. Webb, board supervisor and college coach, using college equipment
9) Bowling – Need bus – Mrs. McBrine – bowling alley
10) Frisbee Throwing – Miss Dye – playground area behind the pool
11) Softball – Miss Weaver and Mrs. Lane – at softball field
12) Baseball – Mr. Martin and Mr. Melton – at Middle School baseball field
13) Soccer – Ms. Browning and Mrs. Kiser – at Middle School soccer field
14) Badminton – Mr. Facemyer – handball court 1 nearby in old grocery store turned gym
15) Volleyball – Mrs. Keathley – handball court 2 in old grocery store turned gym
16) Handball – need bus – Mrs. Brown – handball court 3 in old grocery store turned gym
17) Skateboarding – Mr. Smith – need bus – at the skateboarding park
18) Gymnastics – Miss Perry – need bus – at gymnastics gym
19) Cheerleading – Mrs. Rogers – church gym
20) Dancing – Mrs. Murphy – on the stage in the auditorium
21) Hiking – Need bus – Miss Marino – woods behind park
22) Trampolining – need bus – Ms. Hunter – gymnastics gym
23) Wrestling – Mr. Lyons – handball court 4 in old grocery store turned gym
24) Weightlifting – Mr. Crawford – weight room
25) Tricycling – Mrs. Parrish – school hallway
26) Archery – Mr. Walton – field behind girls' gym
27) Golf – Need school van – Mr. Rogers – to golf course
28) Horseback Riding – Need bus – Miss Bailes – to state park

Chapter 13

One morning, Zane was selling some more of his 'magic pops' to both Deuce and Liv. He saw Konnor getting off the bus, so he went to talk with her. Zane finally got to ask Konnor if she had heard about his 'magic pops.' When she said yes, Zane asked if she wanted to buy some, and Konnor agreed.

Later, in class, Konnor started to sign up for swimming, but at the last minute she crossed it out and signed up for gymnastics. After all, that was the only sport she truly loved. Plus, she was going to get some of Zane's 'magic pops.'

The other students in Mrs. Williams class signed up for:

1) Tiffany – dance
2) Alexandra – swimming
3) Zane – football
4) Hannah –track and field
5) Grace – ice skating
6) Hayden – golf
7) Paul – track and field
8) Emma -- rowing
9) Corwin -- archery
10) Lorinda -- soccer
11) Cole -- football
12) Liv -- softball
13) Deuce -- baseball
14) Joelyn – table tennis

While the students were signing up for their field day sports, Mrs. Williams noticed that Cole seemed very sad and was not participating like he always did. Usually, Cole was such a happy student who always tried to make other students laugh with his pranks. Mrs. Williams asked Cole what was wrong. She was sure he was just not feeling well. Instead, Cole told Mrs. Williams that his aunt in Michigan had gone to a store. She had found a bottle of cinnamon syrup. Now, when he was older, he couldn't take credit for his invention. Mrs. Williams told Cole that he had plenty of other ideas. She said it was a compliment that he had come up with such a great idea at 3 years of age, and that it was the same idea that someone else had who was much older than he was. She told him she was proud of him, and then wrote on the board a common saying: GREAT MINDS THINK ALIKE! Tiffany said, "That's what my mom said to my grandpa when he bought me the same birthday gift that I had just gotten from my dad." Tiffany just shared the toy her dad gave her with her brother and took the one her grandpa gave her and told him, "I love it!" She was glad to have a second one because now she and her brother could play together. She really did love it.

Chapter 14

Just before field day, Mrs. Williams was about to go to her classroom when she happened to see Zane and Corwin talking in the hall. Then she saw him taking money from Corwin and giving him what Zane called 'magic pops.' She knew she had to have a talk with Zane, but right now she had to set up for class.

Konnor was excited about field day because she liked to play games. Although gymnastics was her favorite sport, she enjoyed watching games, and playing outdoor games and board games. She always played to win and was usually successful. Her least favorite games to play were video games. Still, she often played with her brother who could easily beat her. That is probably why video games were her least favorite, although she did like them. Konnor really didn't mind losing to him because he was very good.

Playing games outside with her friends from the neighborhood or during recess was fun for Konnor. They usually played Tag, Hide and Seek, Red Rover, or SPUD. All the air and exercise made her feel so alive!

Sometimes, when Konnor had time to watch TV, she would watch the game show channel. She was pretty good at answering the questions on those shows.

Christmas at her grandma's house was a lot of fun. After the big meal and opening gifts, they played games. First, they always played bingo where with every win, they got to choose a prize of their choice. Konnor was sure her grandmother had bought certain gifts just for her to choose, like a stack of canvases. There were also gifts that several people would want, so the competition began to see who would call bingo first and get the prize everyone wanted.

The games they played after that were different each year, and they were always fun. One year they played Go to the Center. Another year, they played Win with Heads or Tails. Konnor and her cousins always looked forward to whatever games her grandmother planned.

Board games were Konnor's favorite to play. She was in a board game group that met once a week. Points were awarded for each win with 5 points for 1st place, 3 points for 2nd place, and 1 point for 3rd place. She didn't get to go to the group meetings often, but if members played with family or friends during the week, they could also win points. Her favorite game was Train Riding because no one could beat her. But... she had never played with Corwin.

One of Konnor's favorite days in Mrs. Williams' class was the one day each year when they got to play a board game. Everyone in the school knew about her board game day. Even students in other classes who liked to play board games would ask about what game they got to play and who won.

Mrs. Williams would pick a game that she thought no one had ever played. Her students had to read the rules and figure out how to play without help. The game always went along with whatever they were studying. When they were studying about a country, the game originated in that country.

The gifted class for first and second graders was on Monday, and Mrs. Williams was the teacher for that class too. Konnor had been in that class for the last two years and was always the winner. She thought it was one of the most fun days of the year. Many of her classmates agreed.

Since it was close to the end of the year and they hadn't had a board game day, Konnor wondered if Mrs. Williams had this activity for her Tuesday classes too. She also thought about getting to play Cole's Mexican Jumping Beans game. She didn't think that would count because it was in his presentation, and they only played for a few minutes. She remembered that they played hockey when they studied Canada, but that was to study the physics of the game. Surely that didn't count.

Since most of the rest of the year was to be spent planning and then going to field day, Konnor thought there would be no board game day for the Tuesday gifted class. So, Konnor was surprised, as were her classmates, when Mrs. Williams first updated the class on the planning of the field day, then told the class that she had decided that since the planning was going so well, they should take a break from the planning and have a board game day. Konnor was so happy to be wrong!

Mrs. Williams explained that this board game day would be a little different from those of the past. She had not one, but nine sports games from which they could choose. All the games were for ages 8 and above or 10 and above. Groups were to form and play as many games as possible during the day. She thought each group would probably only get to play about seven of the nine games unless they had trouble with the directions.

First, she wanted to know if anyone had played any of these games because if they had, she wanted to take that game out of play. To her surprise, no one had played any of them. "Corwin are you sure? I know your mom helps plan gaming events all over this country and you play a lot of games, which is why I brought so many."

Corwin assured Mrs. Williams he had never played any of the games she brought. He didn't usually play sports games.

Student groups were formed, and they began to select the first game they wanted to play. They had to read the rules carefully and with no help learn how to play each game. Choices were:

1) Blitzing, about football
2) Tricky Shooting about hockey
3) Freshwater Flying Highs about fishing
4) Paris Biking about bicycle racing
5) Baseball Hits about baseball
6) Rugby Crashing about rugby
7) Fast Camels about camel racing
8) Jabbing Your Opponent about boxing
9) Ski Runs and Bloopers about skiing

That afternoon, when the results of the day listed on the board were tallied, students were surprised. In the first group, Tiffany was the winner with 4 of the 7 games played. In the second group, Paul had also won 4 of the 7 games played. In the third group, Lorinda won 3 games, but her group only finished 6 games. In the 4th group, Konnor won all but one of the 7 games they played. But in the 5th group, Corwin had won all 7 of the games they played!

Even though she knew that Corwin was good at playing games, Konnor was surprised that he beat her. The whole class was surprised. Konnor was a graceful loser though. She gave Corwin a high-five. Then the rest of the class followed her lead and gave him a high-five too. He was not in her board gaming group, but she wanted to invite him to join. Maybe she should just invite anyone in the class who was interested in joining. Some of the second-place winners, and even others who were good players, might enjoy her board gaming group. She decided that her board gaming group would be the real winners since they would have more people to play games. Konnor also had to admit that she had so much fun today even though she didn't win.

As they were leaving, Mrs. Williams complimented Alexandra on her newspaper article. She had mentioned all the sports the students would be playing during the field day. She wrote about the class's planning, and how so many people from the community had been willing to help make this day promising.

Mrs. Williams reminded her students that they would continue with the last-minute planning for field day next week. Then, she told Zane she wanted to talk to him after class.

GREAT MIN
THINK ALIK

Chapter 15

When all the other students were gone, Mrs. Williams asked Zane about his 'magic pops.' Zane turned red. He didn't know she knew about them, but he knew he had been caught.

"I just wanted to help my friends do better in their games. They do their best when they are sure they can do it," said Zane.

"Tell the truth. Is that the only reason?" asked Mrs. Williams.

"No," said Zane as he hung his head. "It was for me too, so I could help my mom pay for her medicine."

Mrs. Williams gave Zane a hug. "I thought so."

Zane confessed, "I know it was wrong. I just needed to help my mom, and I thought I could also help my friends."

"Zane, did you know it's against the rules to sell things at school unless it's for the school with the school board saying it's okay?" Mrs. Williams asked him. "Even more importantly, you should never sell students something that they could eat, especially if they look like pills! Not to mention that you knew it was wrong."

"I'm sorry, Mrs. Williams," Zane muttered.

"You knew your 'magic pops' didn't work, but you lied to your friends who believed they would work, didn't you?" Mrs. Williams asked. As Zane nodded, Mrs. Williams continued, "You could be in serious trouble. I know you would never hurt anyone on purpose. You always try to help everyone because you are a friend to all. However, you must set everybody straight. You must do what is called 'atone' for what you did. You must make it right. How do you think you could do that?"

"I guess I could tell everyone that I sold my 'magic pops' the truth," Zane replied. "Would I still get into trouble if I do that?"

"Zane, that's exactly what you must do. I'll make you a deal. If you tell all the kids to whom you sold your candy, I will see you don't get into big trouble. But you need to do this as soon as possible."

"I'll start finding everyone today. Thank you for helping me not get into big trouble. I'll tell them all the truth," Zane said gratefully.

Zane gave Mrs. Williams a hug as she then told him, "Not only that, if your mom agrees, I'll even let you help Sarah, Sam, and me with some yard work. I'm sure it will bring you more money than selling 'magic pops.'"

Chapter 16

Zane began by telling Deuce and Liv the truth about his 'magic pops.' They were his first customers. They were surprised as they had been doing well in every game since Zane had sold them the 'magic pops'. Zane assured them it was their talent and just knowing that they could do it. When they believed in themselves, they could do anything. Liv said, "I guess you're right." Deuce agreed, "I did go into the games just knowing that I could play well."

Zane found several of the students who bought the candy from him and believed his lies. When he told them the truth, just like Deuce and Liv, almost all of them were surprised that the 'magic pops' didn't work as they were doing well in their sports. A few of them were sad at first to find out the truth. Three of his friends were standing together when Zane told them the truth. One of them got mad because he had lied to them and taken their money. The other two actually started to laugh because even if the candy wasn't supposed to help them, it did. One of them said, "I got my money's worth." Then, the kid who had been mad had to agree and joined in the laughter. When Zane asked him if he wanted his money back, he said no. "I guess I got my money's worth too."

By the morning of the field day, Zane had told everyone but Konnor the truth. He couldn't find her because she was late coming to school and had gone straight to the bus going to the gym. He would just have to tell her when her bus returned.

Chapter 17

The most fun day of the year was here at long last! Mrs. Williams was happy that all the jobs her students had listed for the field day had been completed. She was pleased with all the work her students had done to make this a successful day. Each of her students who were not riding a bus that day had a special job for the day. For example, Liv greeted parents as they arrived, giving them name tags and telling them where to go. Deuce was the lookout for the buses. Paul and Zane took the lunch crates to the buses. Cole was on the intercom to announce which sport was dismissed, with students going on the buses dismissed first. Lorinda and Tiffany were trouble shooters before the field day got started.

During the day, a few of the students began to hear rumors about some things that happened during the field day. Some were funny and some were not.

When the buses began arriving back to the school at the end of the field day events, they dropped the students off at a different door, the one closest to where the assembly was taking place. Zane was in the wrong place and missed Konnor. He didn't see her until she was inside the assembly, and he couldn't talk to her there.

Mrs. Williams met the mayor, told him of a few of the funny things that had happened during the day. A few students who saw the mayor and knew him also told him about their day when he asked. After the students were all seated, Mrs. Lohan called the students to order and told them that Mrs. Williams had a few words for them. She told them about how hard her students had worked to plan the field day and hoped that everyone had enjoyed themselves. Mrs. Williams then added that the mayor was able to be here and thanked Corwin for asking his father to come and "who, of course, couldn't say no to his son." Then, she introduced the mayor.

The mayor began talking about what a privilege it was for him to be there, and for all the students to have the opportunity to spend the day playing sports. "It should count as P.E. time. This is a day of fun for students, but it is also a learning day. We learn about winning and losing and being good sports. Some of you may have learned about a sport you have not ever played before. Some of you got to play your favorite sport. Whatever you did today, I hope you had fun!" After a few more words, he began to talk about the day's events. He then spent several minutes discussing all the mishaps of the day.

The mayor began to tell what he had been told about the day, "Some of you haven't heard about many of the things that happened today. Let me be the first to tell you that some things went a little haywire. A couple of the buses were late and the van taking the golf team wouldn't start. The middle school saved the day by letting the elementary use their van. Yeah, middle school."

"Then things only went downhill when the office got a call from the kitchen and the fire alarm went off. There was a small fire in the kitchen that set off the alarm. That meant that students in the building had to evacuate for a few minutes while the fire department was called. They made sure the fire was put out and everything was safe for students to go back into the school. Fortunately, lunch was still served at the scheduled time for each sport."

"Now those things could happen, and the rest of the day could go well. But not today. This day quickly turned into a wacky field day. I will tell you a few stories. There were quite a few student bloopers that happened today. While I'm going to mention several students in different classes by name, I'm going to mostly tell on Mrs. Williams' students because they did the planning, learning great leadership skills, to make this day happen."

"Lorinda was playing goalie in soccer and about to keep the other team from getting a goal, but a dog named Max ran onto the field trying to get the ball, and that dog tripped her. She fell on her face and the dog must have been really scared. The dog stopped, looked at Lorinda, and then ran away as fast as it could. Sorry, Lorinda. Glad you didn't get hurt. My guess is that Max, who is a good dog, changed his mind about wanting that ball when he saw you fall."

"You won't believe what I heard about next. On the volleyball team was a girl named Jessica. She must be able to twist her body like nobody, but maybe a circus entertainer, could do. She thought the ball was going behind her, so she turned to watch where it landed. Somehow the ball landed on her back just as she was bending over a little. Don't know how she did it, but she managed to lift her body so that the ball went back over the net. I don't think anybody in the world of volleyball has ever seen a shot like that. I bet colleges in her future will want her but will have to compete with the circus to get her."

"My favorite story was about a football game because I'm such a fan of that sport. Cole and Zane were playing on opposite sides in the football game. Cole had never played on that field before. He got confused. When he caught the ball, he ran for a touchdown, but he ran the wrong way. He scored a touchdown for the other team. But that wasn't all. I understand that Zane felt bad for Cole because his teammates were giving Cole such a hard time. So, after a few plays, when Zane got the ball, he ran the wrong way and scored for Cole's team. Zane told me he thought it was only fair. It was like starting at a zero score again instead of 6-6. Now they could find out which team was really the best."

"Paul is a top racer. His dad is the coach of the middle school track team, so Paul often goes there after school and practices with the team. Today, during one of the events, he was sprinting around the track. The guy in front of him, River, was in first place when he stumbled. Paul hopped right over him as did four other guys. That guy gets up, unharmed, and continues the race, although now in last place. Paul thought he had won the race as he was now in first place, but then over his shoulder he sees River, the guy who fell and was then in last place. River passed Paul and won the race by inches. Way to go, River! What a race! Tough luck, Paul."

"Hannah also was with the track and field group. She was jumping hurdles when she missed getting over one. I understand that Hannah wants to go into medicine and is always thinking about health and safety. It's a good thing that she had suggested volunteers for the nurse's station since she was the one of the ones who most needed them today for her scraped knee."

"During the morning archery practice, they used balloons as targets. Corwin's arrows kept hitting the string holding the balloon to the board instead of hitting the balloon and breaking it, so his practice score wasn't very good. Corwin is usually very good at archery. He loves this sport and is quite good with his aim. By the way, he did have the highest score for the archery competition during the field day event though. Congratulations!"

"One of our students named Nick wanted me to tell you about his bowling trip today. He dropped the ball, and it went backwards. When he went to pick the ball back up, he fell on top of it. Luckily, he wasn't hurt. Nick has a good sense of humor. He just laughed saying that at least the ball didn't go in the gutter. Nick, I'll take you bowling again whenever your mom says it's okay. That ball is heavy. I'd like to see how you make it go backwards."

"Tiffany went dancing. She has taken lessons since she was just a toddler. She is so graceful and was happy to be learning a new move during today's practice. Then, she bent over and ripped her tights. Since she didn't have any other clothes there, she had to sit out for part of the day until her mom could leave work and bring her more clothes. Tiffany, you should have called me. I would have been happy to bring you a pair my daughter's tights, and I could have been there in ten minutes."

"Emma was rowing with a group at our nearby local college. She lost her paddle in the water. When she tried to get it back, she fell into the water. It's lucky that she is such a good swimmer. I guess you needed extra clothes too. Maybe everyone needs to bring extra clothes to next year's field day."

"When Deuce was up to bat in his baseball game, he hit the ball. However, it was a foul ball that hit a car's front windshield and cracked it. Whose car? The principal's car. You better believe that Mrs. Lohan moved her car to another parking space. Deuce was having a bad day, but he thought his luck had changed when he was up to bat a little later in the game. He hit the ball over the fence. A home run with the bases loaded! However, the ball landed on the newly parked back window of the principal's car! Now she must fix two windows. Mrs. Lohan I hope you have good insurance, and Deuce, I hope you told her you were sorry."

"I heard Liv hit the ball in her softball game, but she threw the bat again. I've heard she's known for that. This time it hit the umpire. He wasn't hurt. Did you know that the umpire doesn't get to walk to first base and be the ump there when the ball hits him? By the way, she wasn't ejected from the game this time."

"I heard Joelyn had never played table tennis before, but she wanted to learn. On the very first serve, the ball hit her in the eye. She didn't complain much, but later it happened again. Only this time the ball hit her in the other eye. By the time a couple more games were over, she thought her eyes had begun to swell and blacken. She went to see the nurse who gave her ice for her eyes. Joelyn told everyone that she was sure she looked like a raccoon. Her eyes aren't as bad as she thought, but if they were, I believe you would be the cutest racoon ever seen."

"I heard Grace went ice skating today. She had on a scarf that dropped. As she tried to go around her scarf, she bumped into Rowan. That caused her to fall into a beautiful split on the ice right in front of him. Although it was a nice split, I guess Grace didn't feel very graceful, especially when he fell on top of her. Then came along Aayla who fell on top of them and then two more kids. All this time, Grace was still in her split. I am surprised she was able to get up and skate away after the rink skaters helped the pile of her friends get off top of her. Without the rink skaters' help, she might still be under that pile." The students giggled as they thought about the picture that pile made.

"For some of you, bad luck followed you all day. Hayden, I am talking about you. Talk about wacky! Hayden was having a terrible day. He hit his golf ball into the lake 3 times, but that was not all. He also hit it into a sand trap. Fortunately, he was not the worst player on the trip. Someone, not mentioning any name, scored worse than he did."

"No one from Mrs. Williams' class went fishing, but a child that I spoke to before this assembly wanted me to tell his story. The child is named Joe, and he caught a monster fish. Now Joe is a little guy and the fish was so big that it pulled him into the water. It's good that his dad was one of our PTA volunteers and went with the group for this activity. His dad jumped in to pull his son out of the water. Little Joe told me he is sad that he lost his fish. No, he wasn't sad he fell in and got wet, just sad that he lost his fish."

"Alexandra is a top swimmer on the swim team. She wins first place in all her swim meets, but as she was swimming in the deep end today, she got severe stomach cramps. She went under and the lifeguard had to save her. I'm glad he saved you. Not only did we not want you to drown, we don't want the other teams to win this summer."

"Now I understand that Cole has a cousin. He introduced his cousin, Bunky, to me. Now for those of you who don't know Bunky, he is a tall kid. He told me that when he was playing basketball, he tried to dunk the ball. After he came back down from his jump, he landed on another kid on his team, Walker. He landed partly on Walker's head and partly on his shoulders, with a leg on each side of his head. He showed me a picture his mom took with her cell phone. Bunky, I'm thinking you could join a stunt performing basketball team and earn money doing that for crowds of people."

"And speaking of Walker, I understand that when he shot for a basket, the ball hit the rim and came back and hit him smack dab in the head so hard it knocked him to the floor. But being the great athlete he is, he jumped right back up, and continued the game. If it were me, I would have been on that floor for an hour or so, and they would have had to carry me off in a stretcher. Way to go Walker."

"Graig went with the horse-riding group. When he got on the saddle, it was not tightened enough and started to slide to the side of the horse. Luckily, Graig held on tight and the owner of the stables who was nearby ran over to catch him. Graig was able to get off and let them tighten the saddle. But lo, his day of mishaps was not over. They were riding quietly along when a loud noise spooked his horse, and that horse took off like a rocket. Again, the owner who was riding with the group, went after Graig and the runaway horse, saving the day. He may never get on a horse again after all that, but remember the saying about when you fall off a horse, get back on as quickly as possible."

"Jodie was playing badminton when she almost dropped the racket. She saved the day because just as the ball was coming toward her, she grabbed the racket before it fell. The ball hit the handle in just the right way and went back over the net. I think it stunned Jodie as much as it did the other team. They missed the return completely. Score one for Jodie!"

"And for Brian, who dropped his ice cream cone on his shoe, I will buy you one next week. And it will be a super large cone! We hope that one doesn't go kerplunk!"

"There were several other mishaps during the day, but I mostly picked on Mrs. Williams' class and a few more students who asked if I would mention them. I spoke more of her students because we owe them so many thanks. They are the ones who helped with the planning of this wonderful day. What a wacky time! Mrs. Williams told me that she had been teaching gifted students in this small West Virginia town for close to 15 years. She had never seen such craziness or so many mishaps in such a short period of time."

Then, the mayor told the students, "I hope that whether you are having a good day or a bad day, you always just do your best for that day. And now, I think it's time to mention those of you who had a good day today." The mayor went on to recognize the winners of the team sports and individuals who did well, congratulating them for their wins.

At the very end of his speech, the mayor asked Konnor to come shake his hand. As she walked to him, he said, "I bet you thought I forgot you. We are so happy you won the gold again today. I think you are the greatest gymnast our state has ever had, except of course for Mary Lou Retton. You are an inspiration to West Virginia and other young gymnasts. So, today you get the key to our town. This is an honor that we have not given to anyone before, but students, listen well. This will not be the last. You may be the one to get it next year."

Chapter 18

Alexandra knew she could write a great article about this Wacky Field Day. She wouldn't write about all the things that happened. She would only tell a few and omit names unless she had permission. She couldn't wait to get started.

As the students were leaving for home after the assembly, Mrs. Williams saw something that was both bad and good. Emma was about to get on the bus when someone began bullying remarks, and one began rubbing his stomach. Then Zane and a couple of kids from her class spoke up. Her students told the bullies it was not cool to say and do those things and to stop it right now. If they ever saw them bullying again, they would take it to the principal. A few other students joined them telling the bullies how wrong it was. More and more students surrounded Emma to comfort her. The bullies were surprised so many students were calling them down. "The way to end bullying is to not allow it to happen," Mrs. Williams heard someone say. She couldn't have been prouder.

Zane went up to congratulate Konnor and to finally get to talk to her about the 'magic pops.' When he told her the truth, she just shook her head. Zane was confused. He said, "They didn't make you do really well today. You did that on your own. You can do it almost every time if you just start believing in yourself again."

Konnor replied, "You don't understand, Zane." Then she pulled the pops out of her pocket. As she showed them to Zane, she said, "I know. See. I didn't take them today because I knew I didn't need 'magic pops' to do well. I was pretty sure I could win without them." Zane smiled, and as he walked away, Konnor said, "Oh, by the way, a big thanks for telling those bullies to stop because it wasn't cool." Zane's smile turned into a grin.

Chapter 19

The next Tuesday was the last day of school for Mrs. Williams' class for the year. She began class by telling her students how proud she was of them for standing up for Emma. She loved the fact that students in other classes followed their lead and stood up for Emma too.

Mrs. Williams added, "I have something else to say that you need to hear. You should NEVER buy things from someone, be it someone you know or don't know. I know some of you bought 'magic pops,' but that didn't make you do better in your sports." Several of her students turned red. They didn't know Mrs. Williams knew about the 'magic pops.' Zane hadn't told them she knew. She continued, "'Magic pops' are just candy. I'm glad you didn't eat the candy before you went to field day."

"After eating them earlier, some of the children did better in their sports than they had before. The candy probably helped those children do better in their sports because it gave them confidence," Mrs. Williams told her class.

"If any student didn't do as well on their field day event, it was not because he or she didn't eat the candy. It was because that student was just having a bad day. It did turn out to be a Wacky Field Day after all. Bad days happen to everyone sooner or later. Then, Mrs. Williams said, "You just need to believe in yourself." She wrote on the board: BELIEVE IN YOURSELF!

Mrs. Williams congratulated them on doing such a great job with the planning of the field day. She was very proud of them. Of all the things that went wrong, none of them were because of the planning they did. On that last day of class, the students discussed The Wacky Field Day and what they could do to improve it next year.

Then Mrs. Williams got out the buzzer system and her students played trivia. The questions were about everything they had learned the whole year in her class. Paul and Emma both answered the most questions correctly and were declared dual winners. After lunch, there was a party for her students who would not be back in this class next year. This too was something she did every year. Hayden, and Joelyn were 5th graders and would be going to middle school. She told them she would see them there as she was also the teacher of gifted at the middle school. The students knew that Hayden and Grace were twins. Some of them wondered why Grace was not in the 5th grade too. Mrs. Williams explained that after the testing, Hayden wanted to be double promoted. Grace did not. So, their parents had agreed. Hayden would now go on to the 6th grade while Grace stayed in the 5th grade. Emma said, "I always wondered how she could fail a grade and still be in this class. I should have known she didn't fail, he just advanced to a higher grade."

During the party, Mrs. Williams told the class, "Zane is to be congratulated. He helped his mom get the medicine she needed to get well. She is doing much better now, and the doctor said she would be completely cured in just a few weeks. It's like a miracle. When I spoke with her, she also told me some exciting news about Zane. It's like a second miracle for his family. I asked his mom if I could share this news. She agreed that I could tell you about her getting better and Zane's good news. Most of you know that Zane has had a couple of small parts in movies. He has also played a few major roles in our community theater productions. What most of you don't know is that he got a call from a producer/director two nights ago. They want him to star in a TV series starting soon. Unfortunately for us, but happy for Zane, he will be moving to Los Angeles, California sometime this summer. He promises to let us know when it will begin to air on TV so we can all watch it." The students all clapped with excitement for their classmate.

Mrs. Williams then reminded her students that Konnor was going to begin home school for part of her day so she could train more in gymnastics. She told Konnor, "I hope you can visit our class some of the time, and good luck in your gymnastics."

The last testing to identify gifted students was complete for the year. There would be new students joining the class in the fall. At each meeting, Mrs. Williams was sure to ask the parents if she could tell her class who the students were. When she named Jessica and Jodie, her students were not surprised because they knew how smart these two were. They were the perfect pair since they were best friends. They knew Jessica was hard of hearing and Jodie was really good at sign language.

The third student was Jeff, who was Jessica's cousin. Mrs. Williams told her students that Jeff now went to a nearby school in the county but was moving this summer and would be attending this school in the fall. Because he did his testing in the county, he could begin the year in her gifted class. She hoped they would make him welcome and help him learn about this school.

Next, Mrs. Williams complimented Alexandra on her newspaper article, read it to the class, and gave her a copy. The other students in class also liked it because it was written in such a way that it revealed the bloopers of the day as well as Alexandra's great sense of humor.

Several of the students brought Mrs. Williams a gift to say thank you for the year, and she gave out a few hugs. She also gave each student a small gift bag and she told them not to open it until they got home and showed their parents. She had given them all an invitation to come to a pool party, a candy bar, and a sweet note. With that, Mrs. Williams told them to have a great summer, gave out a few more hugs, wiped away a tear, and said goodbye.

Milton Keynes UK
Ingram Content Group UK Ltd.
UKHW050208211123
432956UK00003B/130